The Dinky Donkey

For Maia. My beautiful girl.
– Craig Smith

To the gorgeously giggling Scottish Granny, who has touched
hearts across the globe with her laughter medicine, reading to the
adorable Archer and inspiring reading aloud to children worldwide.
And to Felicity ... for being sent from heaven.
– Katz Cowley

This edition published in the UK in 2019 by Scholastic Children's Books
Euston House, 24 Eversholt Street, London NW1 1DB
A division of Scholastic Ltd
www.scholastic.co.uk
London – New York – Toronto – Sydney – Auckland – Mexico City – New Delhi – Hong Kong

First published in 2019 by Scholastic New Zealand Limited
Text copyright © Craig Smith, 2019
Illustrations copyright © Katz Cowley, 2019
The moral rights of Craig Smith and Katz Cowley have been asserted.

ISBN 978 1407 19851 4

12

The Dinky Donkey

Words by **Craig Smith**
Illustrations by **Katz Cowley**

Wonky Donkey had a child ...

it was a little girl.

Hee Haw!

She was so cute and small!

She was a **dinky** donkey.

Wonky Donkey had a child,
it was a little girl.

Hee Haw!

She was so cute and small ...

and she had beautiful *long* eyelashes!

She was a
blinky dinky
donkey.

Wonky Donkey had a child,
it was a little girl.

Hee Haw!

She was so cute and small,
she had beautiful long eyelashes ...

and she loved to listen to rowdy music.

She was a **punky** blinky dinky donkey.

Wonky Donkey had a child,
it was a little girl.

Hee Haw!

She was so cute and small,
she had beautiful long eyelashes,
she loved to listen to rowdy music ...

and she painted her hooves bright pink.

She was an
inky-pinky
punky
blinky
dinky donkey.

Wonky Donkey had a child,
it was a little girl.

Hee Haw!

She was so cute and small,
she had beautiful long eyelashes,
she loved to listen to rowdy music,
she painted her hooves bright pink ...

and she had to go pee-pee.

She was a **winky-tinky** inky-pinky
punky blinky dinky donkey.

Wonky Donkey had a child,
it was a little girl.

Hee Haw!

She was so cute and small,
she had beautiful long eyelashes,
she loved to listen to rowdy music,
she painted her hooves bright pink,
she had to go pee-pee ...

and she loved to play the piano.

She was a **plinky-plonky**
winky-tinky inky-pinky
punky blinky dinky donkey.

Wonky Donkey had a child,
it was a little girl.

Hee Haw!

She was so cute and small,
she had beautiful long eyelashes,
she loved to listen to rowdy music,
she painted her hooves bright pink,
she had to go pee-pee,
she loved to play the piano ...

and she wore wild sunglasses.

She was a **funky** plinky-plonky winky-tinky
inky-pinky punky blinky dinky donkey.

Wonky Donkey had a child,
it was a little girl.

Hee Haw!

She was so cute and small,
she had beautiful long eyelashes,
she loved to listen to rowdy music,
she painted her hooves bright pink,
she had to go pee-pee,
she loved to play the piano,
she wore wild sunglasses ...

and she smelt just as bad
as her dad.

She was a **stinky** funky plinky-plonky winky-tinky
inky-pinky punky blinky dinky donkey.

Wonky Donkey had a child,
it was a little girl ...

Hee Hee Hee Haw!